The Invisible Web

by **Patrice Karst**

illustrated by **Joanne Lew-Vriethoff**

Ⓛ Ⓑ

Little, Brown and Company
New York   Boston

ABOUT THIS BOOK: The illustrations for this book were created digitally. This book was edited by Andrea Spooner and designed by Véronique Lefèvre Sweet. The production was supervised by Erika Schwartz, and the production editor was Annie McDonnell. The text was set in Shannon Book, and the display type is Gulyesa Script Regular.

The very best news ever has begun to spread all over the world...
One heart at a time.
Shout it from the mountaintops!
Every single one of us is connected
to those we love by Invisible Strings.

That means Giovanna and her daddy are always together, even though he moved to a new house.

Omar can feel the tugs of love from his parents, even though he is living far away at school.

Mr. Chang still feels Mrs. Chang close by,
even though she died such a very long time ago.

And you, at this very moment, may feel the String of someone close to you, even though they aren't there.

You can't see it, but it's real.

Our Strings reach to everyone we know.

They travel far and wide…to families and friends, classmates and coaches, to bus drivers and babysitters, neighbors and pets, to aunts and uncles and grandparents and grandchildren, and countless other people.

And all of those people have **hundreds of Strings!**

Soaring high over rocky peaks and across the seven seas,

deep into jungles and valleys,

and winding through the busiest of cities...

all these Strings crisscross one another

and create a nest that covers the planet,

interlacing us together, cradling us forever.

The Invisible Web!

The Web has no borders and wraps every continent.
Within it live butterflies and flowers, starfish and seahorses,
lions and ants, rivers and snowstorms, and all human beings:
Giovanna, Omar, Mr. Chang…and, of course, you and me too!

Some say it even reaches to our ancestors and those we cherish in the beyond.
One tug on a String sends love to every one of us woven together in this divine tapestry.
And that means...just one good deed travels across the entire Web.

Everything is linked!

But...sometimes folks forget.
When they can't feel their Strings, they forget about our Invisible Web.
And that's when Strings get tangled up.

Like when lonely Luisa isn't invited to sit with anyone at her school at lunchtime.

Or when sad Stefano wishes his friend Marcos wasn't so bossy when they played.

Or when Mrs. Patel struggles at work without help, and she just wants to quit.

Even violence and war can erupt when too many of us forget the Web.
When Strings are ignored, they can become weak and begin to unravel.

But the more people who care for the Web, the stronger it remains.

The Web feels like every parent since the beginning of time, holding and protecting each one of us in millions of gentle arms. What could be stronger than all those hands holding us close?

So many supportive fingers can always find a way to untangle Strings so that love can flow again.

But it's up to every one of us to spread the word.

Our time is right now.

As we tell our family and friends,
sisters will remind brothers,

who will write to cousins
who will call their great-
grandparents (who will
just nod and smile as if
they have always known).

If we remember the Web, and tug at it often, nobody will ever be left out.
We will see others more clearly.
The people of the world will look into each other's eyes.
They will smile at one another.
And when one of them cries, **they will all want to help.**

And they do!

Marcos apologizes to Stefano, who forgives his friend, and they have even more fun playing.

Someone helps Mrs. Patel at work and tells her what a great job she's doing. She remembers that she's important and feels happy.

And Luisa feels warm and bubbly inside when a few of the kids in class ask her to join them under the banyan tree for lunch. She knows right then that **the Invisible Web is real.**

After school, Luisa cries with joy as she strokes her cat,
who purrs the news to the stars.
And the stars whisper the secret to the clouds,
who share it with the songbirds,

who serenade the world with this exquisite melody of love
at the start of each morning and all during the day...
until, as the Invisible Web glitters in the magic of twilight,
the owls take over and hoot the news throughout the night:

The Invisible Web is alive!

Its time is right now.
It breathes as we breathe,
pulsating all over our Earth,
the single heartbeat
of life and love.

And do you know what
that makes us all?

One very big family!

P.S.: I just love being right here in the very middle of the Invisible Web, with you....

—Patrice Karst

*Dedicated to the REAL
worldwide Web*